This book belongs to

_____

_____

_____

For Pau and Mar

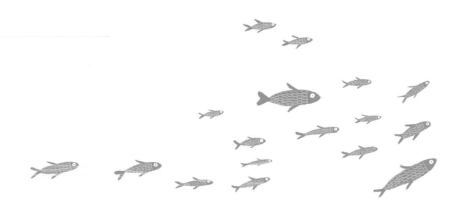

Tales from the Hidden Valley: Under the Water © Flying Eye Books 2019

First edition published in 2019 by Flying Eye Books,
an imprint of Nobrow Ltd. 27 Westgate Street, London E8 3RL.

Text and illustrations © Carles Porta 2019

Translation by Lawrence Schimel

Published in the US by Nobrow (US) Inc.

Printed in Latvia on FSC® certified paper.

ISBN: 978-1-911171-68-3

FSC
www.fsc.org

MIX
Paper from
responsible sources
FSC® C002795

www.flyingeyebooks.com

Tales from the Hidden Valley

Under the Water

Carles Porta

Flying Eye Books
London | New York

Hidden far away between tall mountains, there lies a secret valley. You could pass it a hundred times and still not see it, unless you knew just where to look...

Summer was about to arrive in the valley. As they did every year, the inhabitants whispered fanciful tales into the warm night air and slept under the stars, because tomorrow they would celebrate 'DRAGON'S DAY'!

According to legend, in the deepest part of
the lake lives an enormous and terrible dragon,
who sleeps upon a glittering pile of treasure.

If someone is unfortunate enough to wake him,
the dragon emerges, breathing a fire so fierce
that it lights up the whole valley. In celebration
of this legend, a festival is held every year.

Every Dragon's Day, a strange being
also emerges from the lake...

...who looks just like a mermaid. Despite her
youthful face, she is as old as the legend
of the dragon itself. Her name is Aqua.

Aqua spied on the festival preparations from afar.
She felt so different from the others, and lived
among them like a ghost that no one could see.

Seeing how time passed so quickly for everyone
but her, Aqua decided she would preserve the
inhabitants' things for ever and keep them safe.

Moving stealthily,
Aqua took a book
from Yula...

...the rockets
for the fireworks...

...and some
fossils that Sara
had found.

Max the trumpeter had come to the valley last winter. Since then, he'd set out to meet each and every one of its inhabitants.

"Who is this new person?" he wondered.

Aqua was just as surprised to encounter Max, and she angrily splashed him with water!

Eventually seeing the funny side, Aqua
laughed harder than she had in a long
time, and she was delighted when Max
sent a jet of water right back at her.

Aqua felt something unknown until then. For the first time in her long and solitary life, she invited someone to her strange underground home.
"It has stunning views of the lake," she told Max.

Max was having such a good time he didn't pay much attention to the objects that lay around Aqua's home. He was more occupied with the algae tea, which turned his nose green!

Meanwhile, the inhabitants of the valley
were unsettled by the latest series of thefts...

...and they decided once and for all to find out who was responsible.

Yula, Sara and Ticky set out to investigate. Yula couldn't understand why someone might take someone else's things and she was in a very foul mood indeed.

When Onion-head saw Yula approaching, she was frightened and decided to hide.

Chasing after her, the friends were surprised
to discover the secret entrance to a tunnel!
It must have been as old as the valley itself.

As they wandered deeper inside, they found themselves in an immense cave. They walked in the darkness between mountains of new and ancient things.

Coming from somewhere at the back, there was a light and some music.

Meanwhile, Max and Aqua
were having a ball together.

Suddenly the music stopped and there was a long silence. Yula was furious. There, lying on the ground, was her book, the rockets and Sara's rocks.

And who should be there but Max and a very strange-looking girl!

Yula began to demand explanations.
Aqua's face turned redder than a pepper.

She was very upset. In two steps, Aqua disappeared
behind the curtain of water that led out into the lake.

Aqua's head grew hot, as if it had a fire inside.
Not even the cool water of the lake could calm it.

Her anger and sadness grew so strong that without
being able to avoid it she decided to seek revenge!

Suddenly, the group began to hear the
sound of snoring coming from the lake.
Who could be making such an awful noise?

Aqua swam down, down, down. It was so dark and calm at the bottom of the lake that hardly a single sound could reach there and wake the enormous dragon who slept peacefully.

Unless someone decided to wake him up.

Just at the last moment, and with a tremendous effort, Aqua managed to stop the shout that was about to escape her throat.

She'd had such a nice time today, and at
last she had a friend. If Aqua awoke the fury
of that beast, she'd be alone once more.

Sara followed the sound of the snoring deep into the cave. There, buried among many other things, she came across a small submarine in the shape of a fish.

Its name was Olivier.

Olivier was the most incredible machine she'd ever seen. Sara was desperate to take him for a ride.

Yula didn't want Max to be mad at her for treating his friend so poorly, and she knew Olivier was the perfect way to find Aqua ... so the group set out.

Olivier illuminated the dark waters with his bright lights, casting a warm glow over the shadows.

Finally, Max saw Aqua,
who was asleep on
a bed of seaweed.

He was so happy to see her that without thinking, he tooted a great big 'HELLO!' on his trumpet.

The dragon awoke in an instant!

Startled by the noise, Olivier took off across the lake ... straight towards the mouth of the enormous beast who lay waiting for them.

The group disappeared in one giant gulp.

On the shore of the lake, the inhabitants
sat awaiting the firework display.

Despite nobody knowing where the rockets
were, everyone trusted that as soon as
it got dark, there would be a celebration.

Inside the dragon's stomach, Olivier's passengers tried not
to panic. They searched every corner of the submarine
looking for anything that might save them...

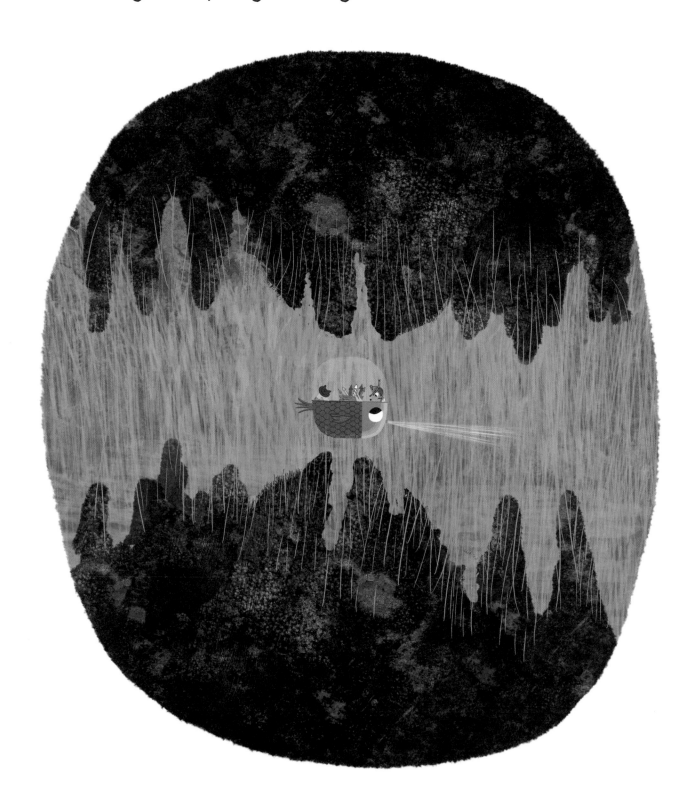

...and then Onion-head found the fireworks.

Emerging from the water, the dragon spluttered and spewed a rainbow of sparks. The spectators stared with their mouths agape.

Olivier was expelled from the dragon's mouth
and crossed the sky in a magnificent arc. From up
in the air, the friends waved to everybody below.

That Dragon's Day had been so special it
would be remembered in the valley for a long
time. And the inhabitants now had a new
friend to share the celebrations with – Aqua.

After summer, autumn would return and Aqua would disappear beneath the lake's cold waters once more ... or perhaps not this time ... but that is for another story.